Luna's
First Garden Adventure

Chris Maxwell

Balboa Press books may be ordered through booksellers or by contacting:

Balboa Press
A Division of Hay House
1663 Liberty Drive
Bloomington, IN 47403
www.balboapress.co.uk
UK TFN: 0800 0148647 (Toll Free inside the UK)
UK Local: 02036 956325 (+44 20 3695 6325 from outside the UK)

ISBN: 978-1-9822-8532-6 (sc)
ISBN: 978-1-9822-8531-9 (e)

Print information available on the last page.

Balboa Press rev. date: 04/08/2022

BALBOA.PRESS
A DIVISION OF HAY HOUSE

To

Ann Marie (Bodo!)
So proud of you.
x

Luna's
First Garden Adventure

Cris Maxwell
& Luna!

"Luna had never been outside before... And the garden looked ENORMOUS.

She peeped out from behind the patio door and jumped with fright when a voice meowed.

"Hello, I'm Poppy. Why don't you come outside and play in the garden with me?"

"I have a tummy ache today, maybe I'll come out tomorrow," said Luna shyly.

"I get tummy aches too when I'm scared. The garden looks big but it's so much fun and I know something that will help," said Poppy.

3

"You need to breathe like this...

"Take a deep breath right up your nose and then blow it out gently down through your toes."

"That's silly," said Luna. "You don't breathe through your toes and anyway we have paws not toes!"

"I know that," replied Poppy. "But it's just a little rhyme to teach you how to breathe more slowly. Try it."

Luna copied Poppy and started to feel a bit better. "Do it again," meowed Poppy.

So Luna took a long, deep breath in, and as she breathed out she imagined it going slowly all the way down her body. It definitely helped!

Then she bravely put her tiny paws onto the tickly grass.

It felt very strange at first, not at all like the fluffy carpet or the smooth kitchen floor.

But soon she was running all over the garden with Poppy.

The kittens had so much fun together. Until...

Luna got so excited. She climbed HIGH up a tree and onto the garden shed... and then she was STUCK!

"Breathe!" yelled Poppy.

"Take a deep breath right up your nose and then blow it out gently down through your toes!"

The garden looked a long way down and Luna was scared. Her little legs felt wobbly and she felt all hot inside. She thought she was going to fall but she listened to Poppy and did the special breathing. Then...

She jumped down from the shed, landing on a big shiny stone...

What a fright she got...
and so did Tootles the tortoise!

"Oops, sorry," said Luna. "I didn't mean to give you a fright.

Would you like to play with me and my friend Poppy?"

Tootles, Poppy and Luna had so much fun.

Luna forgot all about feeling scared as she played with her new friends. She didn't even realise how tired and hungry she was until she heard her name being called from the house.

She waved goodbye to both Poppy and Tootles as she hurried inside.

Luna was very happy to see her favourite supper waiting for her. She was so hungry she gobbled it up as fast as she could.

And then, curling up in her basket, she...

Took a deep breath right up her nose and blew
it out gently down through her toes... Zzzzzz

And, if you ever feel worried or scared, you can try Luna's special breathing, too. Why don't you try it now...

Take a deep breath right up your nose and blow it out gently down through your toes.

Chris Maxwell 2022

Lightning Source UK Ltd.
Milton Keynes UK
UKHW050850190422
401710UK00005B/13